Fly Free!

Roseanne Thong

ILLUSTRATED BY

Eujin Kim Neilan

BOYDS MILLS PRESS
Honesdale, Pennsylvania

For Maya and all others who turn the circle of kindness
—R.T.

For my mother, Uckang Namkoong
—E.K.N.

The author offers sincere thanks to Huong Diep Dao for her insight into Vietnamese culture, and to Jin Rou, Dharma Realm Buddhist University, and San-pao Li, Ph.D., professor emeritus, California State University, Long Beach, for their guidance on the Buddhist beliefs of karma and nirvana.

Text copyright © 2010 by Roseanne Thong
Illustrations copyright © 2010 by Eujin Kim Neilan
All rights reserved

Boyds Mills Press, Inc.
815 Church Street
Honesdale, Pennsylvania 18431
Printed in the United States of America

First edition
The text of this book is set in 14-point Adobe Jenson.
The illustrations are done in watercolor on board.

10 9 8 7 6 5 4 3 2

Library of Congress Cataloging-in-Publication Data

Thong, Roseanne.
 Fly free! / Roseanne Thong ; illustrated by Eujin Kim Neilan. — 1st ed.
   p. cm.
 Summary: When Mai feeds the caged birds at a Buddhist temple in Vietnam, her simple act of kindness starts a chain of thoughtful acts that ultimately comes back to her. Includes author's note explaining the Buddhist concepts of karma and samsara, or the wheel of life.
 ISBN 978-1-59078-550-8 (hardcover : alk. paper)
 [1. Kindness—Fiction. 2. Conduct of life—Fiction. 3. Vietnam—Fiction.] I. Neilan, Eujin Kim, ill. II. Title.
 PZ7.T3815Fl 2010
 [E]—dc22
                    2009020248

I**T WAS EARLY MORNING,** and the sun had just risen round and red as a parasol. The earth under Mai's toes was cool, but the sun's first rays cast a warm, golden glow on pagoda eaves. Mai looked for the familiar cage of sparrows for sale by the temple gates.

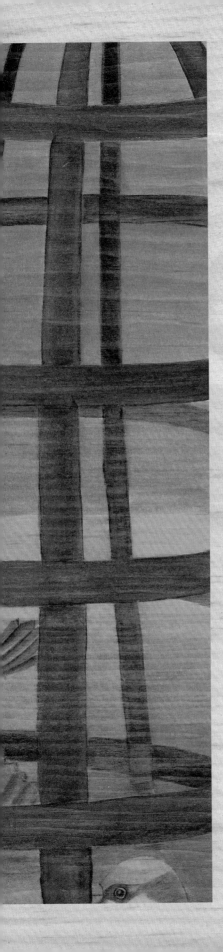

THE BIRDS TWITTERED WITH EXCITEMENT, bobbing their comical heads like tiny puppets.

"May I feed them?" she asked the vendor.

"Of course," he said. "You seem to speak their language!"

As much as Mai loved to visit the birds, she hoped someone would pay for their release. This was the Buddhist way. To set an animal free was a good deed. She would have freed them herself, but the cost was more than her mother could spare.

Mai eased small bowls of seed and water into the cage.

SHUSH-SHUSH, SHUSH-SHUSH. Mai heard the sound of slippers nearby. They were red velvet and belonged to a girl named Thu. When Thu took them off, as was the custom before entering a temple, Mai could not help but stare. She had never seen such a beautiful pair of shoes.

MAI WAITED FOR THU
by the temple door and smiled when she came out.
"The sparrows are hungry," said Mai. "Would you
like to help feed them?"

Thu nodded as Mai poured seed into her
outstretched hand.

Then Mai whispered softly,

"Fly free, fly free,
in the sky so blue.
When you do a good deed,
it will come back to you."

On her way home that day, Thu noticed a girl sitting by the roadside, cradling her foot in her hands. She had been cut by a sharp piece of glass, and the wound stung like an animal's bite.

"My friend!" Thu called to the girl. "Please take these slippers. They'll help ease your pain."

The girl looked up in disbelief. The shoes were the rich,
red color of pomegranates, and the velvet was new and uncrushed.
She put them on and nodded her thanks as Thu sang out,

"Fly free, fly free in the sky so blue. When you do a good deed, it will come back to you!"

The next morning, the girl's foot was much better. One of her daily chores was drawing water from a well at the edge of town. With her new shoes on, she easily shouldered two heavy buckets of cool, spring water that slished and sloshed as she walked.

On the way home, she passed Ong Hai, the oxcart driver, asleep in the shade of a banyan tree. *He'll be thirsty when he wakes up*, she thought. She quietly approached his cart, dipped her coconut shell into the cool, sweet water, and left it on the seat beside him.

When Ong Hai woke up, his throat was parched. To his surprise, a cool drink awaited him. But who had been so kind? Looking down the lane behind him, a girl's song faded into the midday dust . . .

"Fly free, fly free, in the sky so blue. When you do a good deed, it will come back to you!"

Later that day, Ong Hai saw an old woman hobble down the road, balancing a basket of cakes high atop her head.

"Do you need a ride to market?"called Ong Hai.

"Yes," said the woman,"but I have no money."

"Hop in," said Ong Hai."I'll trade a ride for one of your cakes. They look delicious!"

"That they are," the woman replied."I made them myself from an old family recipe."

Ong Hai savored the sweet coconut flavor during the ride to market.
When he left the woman off, he whistled a cheerful tune . . .

"Fly free, fly free, in the sky so blue. When you do a good deed, it will come back to you!"

At market, business was brisk, and the woman soon sold out of cakes. She picked up her empty basket, bought a large sack of rice, and returned home.

The next morning, she awoke to find a lone monk passing her house with his alms bowl in hand. It was breakfast time, and this was the monk's way of asking for food. The woman rushed out to the road with steaming rice for his bowl.

"It's simple but filling," she said.

The monk nodded his thanks, his orange robe streaming behind him like the sun's rays. As he walked off, a song drifted on the morning breeze . . .

"Fly free, fly free, in the sky so blue. When you do a good deed, it will come back to you!"

Touched by these words, the monk went to visit the home of a sick boy in the village. He treated the boy with acupuncture and chanted a river of words. The next day, the child had completely recovered. The happy father went to the temple to give his thanks.

There, by the temple gates, he saw Mai tenderly feeding the sparrows, singing a familiar song:

"Fly free, fly free,
in the sky so blue.
When you do a good deed,
it will come back to you!"

At once, he understood how good deeds are passed from one person to the next. A wheel of kindness existed in people's hearts. It turned day and night, through cities, villages, and countryside, until it came back to its origin, making a full circle.

Without hesitating, he gave the bird owner all the money he had with him.

"I'd like to free the sparrows," he said.

The owner nodded at Mai. Her heart beat like the wings of a thousand birds in flight as she opened the cage door. In a moment, her friends were gone.

Then Mai called out as loudly as she could,

"Fly free, fly free, in the sky so blue. . . ."

AUTHOR'S NOTE

Once, while traveling through Vietnam, I saw a family pay for the release of small birds. A student named Mai described the tradition to me.

"Buddhists believe in reincarnation, or the idea that we are reborn many times," she said. "Our goal is to be reborn as a higher being each time, until we reach what we call *nirvana*, or perfect wisdom."

Mai explained that good or bad actions affect the way we are reborn. She called this *karma*. "When you do a good deed, good karma will return to you," said Mai. "Bad deeds will create bad karma."

Karma can be thought of as a boomerang—our thoughts and actions eventually find their way back home. Buddhists believe that the effects of karma may come now, later in life, or in another life altogether.

Another Buddhist idea is *samsara*, or the wheel of life, as illustrated above, with the story's characters. This ancient Buddhist and Hindu symbol represents the circle of life: birth, death, and rebirth. It also shows how past deeds circle back to affect our present and future.